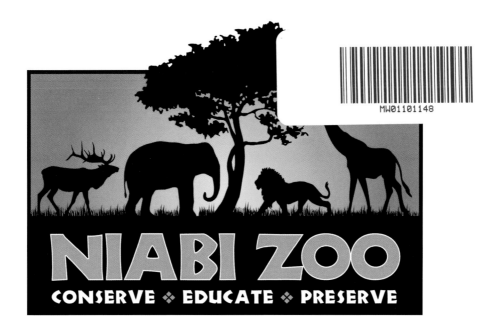

## Foreword by Marc Heinzman

When I was a boy, it seemed there were practically an unlimited number of ways that I could spend the days I wasn't in school. Riding my bike, building forts in the woods, playing baseball, and so many other activities were always good for a fun afternoon, but they could never compete with one activity in particular: going to the zoo. I just couldn't get enough of watching the lions prowl through the grass and the monkeys climb through the branches in their exhibits.

Now as an adult, I have come to know just how great zoos really are. The zoo is the perfect place to see amazing animals from all over the world and learn why it is important to protect them in their wild homes. Zoos play a big part in understanding and protecting rare and fascinating animals found all across the globe.

Visiting your local zoo is a great way to see incredible animals up close, but it's important to remember that while it might seem like a lot of fun to own your very own tiger or rhino, exotic animals require special care and housing. As Blake Ross explains in  the wonderful Why Isn't the Zoo...a Pet Store, Too?, it's best to leave exotic animals to the zoo professionals, but you can do your part by visiting zoos on a regular basis and learning all about animals.

Marc Heinzman - Niabi Zoo

One of our favorite things to do...

Is to visit all the animals at the Zoo.

The Zoo has animals galore...

More than the biggest pet store.

There are so many different kinds to see...

Picking a favorite is too hard for me.

For Zoo Day we're never late...

We get our tickets at the gate.

My mind quickly starts to roam...

How I'd like to take them home.

Even though it's an impossible task...

"Can I have them?" I repeatedly ask.

Mom! Dad! Can I have a pet **Aardvark**... for picnics in the **Park**?

Son. All that ant **Farming**... isn't so **Charming**!

Mom! Dad!
A **Duckbill Platypus** loves to swim...

We can share a pool
with **him!**

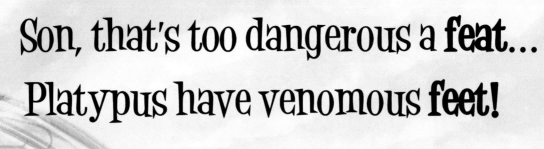

Son, that's too dangerous a **feat**...
Platypus have venomous **feet**!

Mom. Dad.
# Maybe a pet **Flamingo**...
## is the way to **go.**

# Son, Birds of a **feather**... Flock **together**.

That many **birds**... will cause fowl **words**!

Son!
You'll be a nervous **wreck...**

every time you wash his **neck!**

MOM! DAD!

IF I HAD
A PET JACKAL...

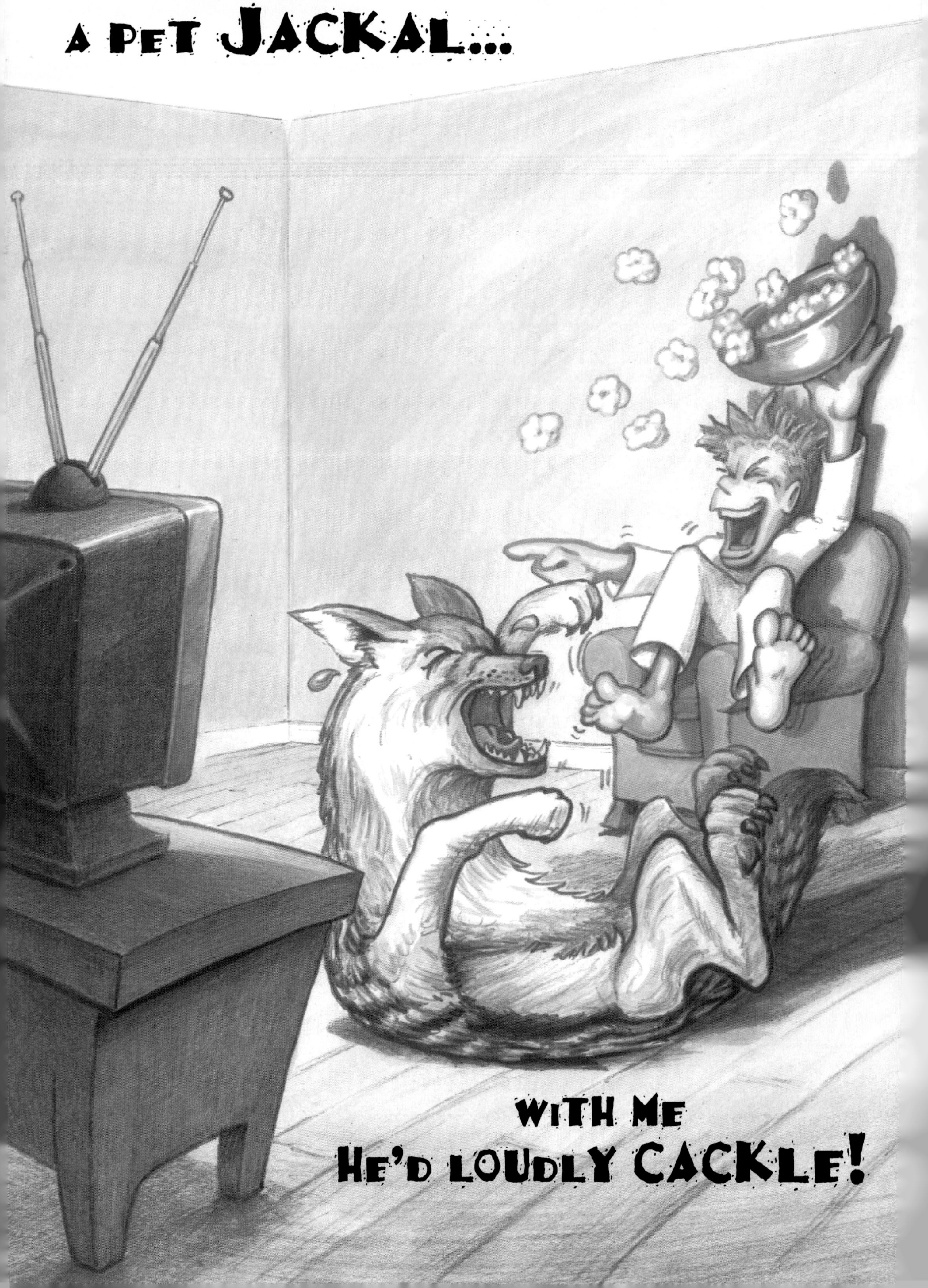

WITH ME
HE'D LOUDLY CACKLE!

Son!

ONCE YOU
GET SLEEPY...

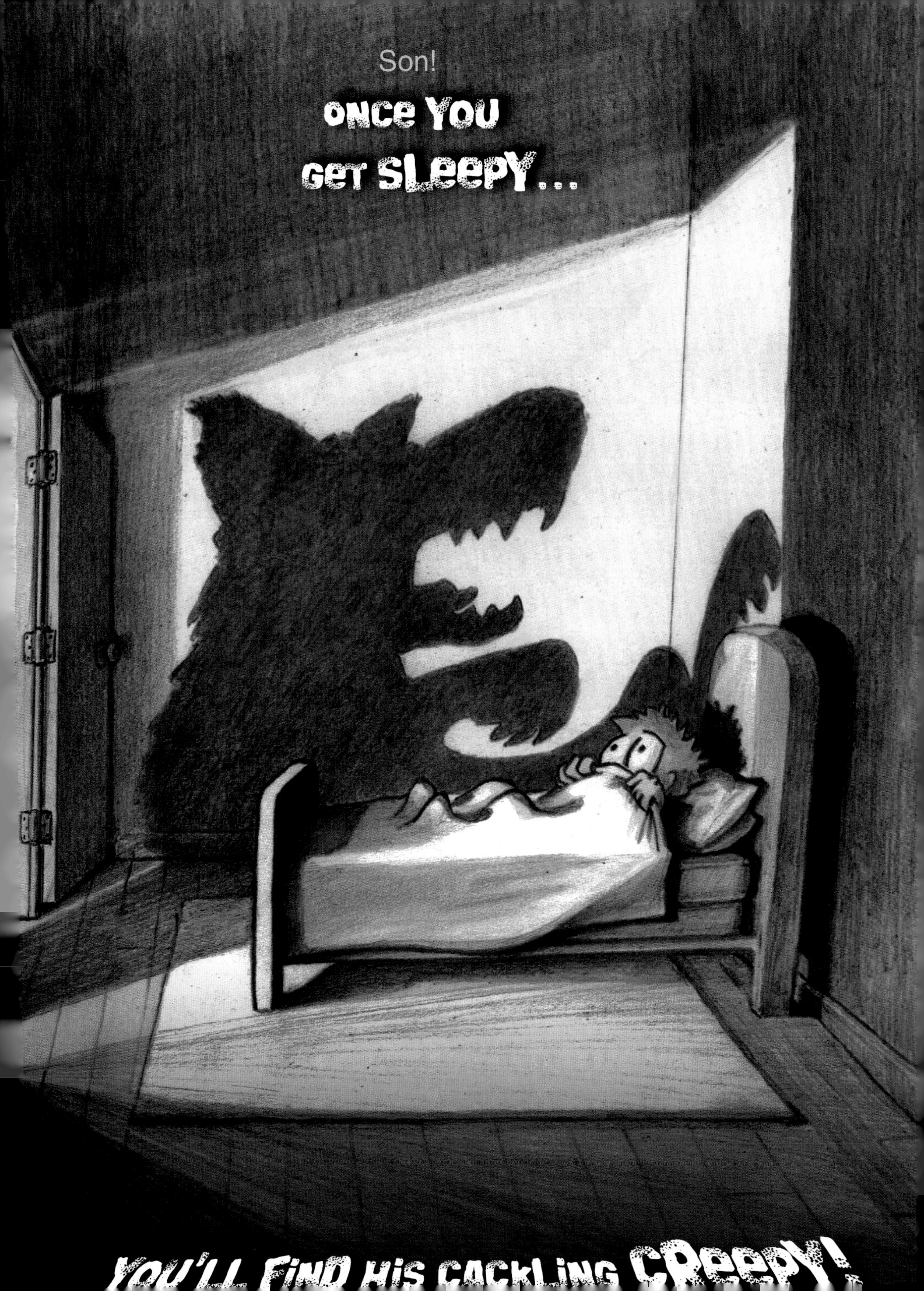

YOU'LL FIND HIS CACKLING CREEPY!

Mom! Dad!
A pet Lion
would rock...

I'd be King
of Our block!

# Hey! Hey! A pet Monkey wins...

# We'd play together like twins!

Mom! Dad!

This little **Numbat** looks **tame**...

what's his undoing **fame?**

Son!
Termites
are his favorite treat...

and our house
is what termites eat!

Mom! Dad!

A pet **Rhino** sure is **NEAT**... He'd be SAFE on any **STREET!**

Yes, Son!

Until some driver makes a **fuss**... Then the FUZZ is chasing **US!**

Mother! Father!.
# A pet **Urubu** King **Vulture**...
## shows I have Royal **Culture!**

Son,
## "Your Royal Laziness" is your **groove**...
## & vultures eat what doesn't **move!**

Mom! Dad!

A **Xenarthra** is an **armadillo**...

He'll *curl up* on my **pillow!**

*Son!*
He *looks like* a little **ball**...
That *problem* isn't so **small!**

He's like all the rest

Living in the Zoo is best

For them this is where it's at

With their family in a proper habitat

Trained Zookeepers, Volunteers & Vet

Making sure all their needs are met

Their Love & Care is Our Responsibility too

Our part is visiting & contributing to our Zoo

THE END